For Finley Rae Hahn

ORCHARD BOOKS

First published in 2015 in the United States by Little, Brown and Company
First published in Great Britain in 2016 by The Watts Publishing Group

3 5 7 9 10 8 6 4 2

A CIP catalogue record for this book is available from the British Library.

ISBN 978 1 40834 206 0

Printed and bound by CPI Group (UK) Ltd, Croydon, CR0 4YY

The paper and board used in this book are made from wood from responsible sources

Orchard Books
An imprint of Hachette Children's Group
Part of The Watts Publishing Group Limited
Carmelite House, 50 Victoria Embankment, London EC4Y 0DZ

An Hachette UK Company

www.hachette.co.uk
www.hachettechildrens.co.uk

Project Funway
Starring Russell Ferguson

Written by Ellie O'Ryan

ORCHARD

 Contents

Chapter 1
A Special Delivery

Bzzz. Bzzz. Bzzz.

Blythe Baxter pulled the pillow over her head.

Bzzz. Bzzz. Bzzz.

What was that buzzing noise?

It wasn't the alarm clock. Today was Saturday; Blythe could sleep in as late as

she wanted.

So what was it?

That's when Blythe noticed her phone, all lit up and buzzing like crazy. The clock on her desk read 2:53 a.m.

Who's calling me in the middle of the night? She pressed the answer button and mumbled, "Hello?"

"Blythe, darling, how are you?"

Blythe sat up straighter, completely wide awake. There was no mistaking that voice – it was the one and only Mona Autumn, publisher of the world-famous fashion magazine *Tres Blasé*.

Blythe had been in awe of her ever since she'd sketched her very first fashion design.

Everybody knew that Blythe loved fashion. But what people didn't know was that she also had a top-secret ability: she could communicate with animals! Blythe and the pets at the Littlest Pet Shop had so many amazing adventures together – including a recent trip to the international Pet Fashion Expo, where Russell the hedgehog had been photographed for *Tres Blasé*!

"I'm calling from Paris with the most fabulous news," Mona said briskly. "Our latest issue of *Tres Blasé* – yes, that's right, the one with you and your prickly pet – has sold more than half a million copies!"

"Half a million copies?" Blythe repeated, in shock.

"And still selling!" Mona crowed. "Needless to say, everyone's thrilled."

"I'm so—" Blythe started, but once more, Mona kept talking.

"And the public! The public is beyond thrilled! What they want, Blythe, is more. More Blythe Style, more fashion hedgehog, more *Tres Blasé*! That's where you come in. We want you and Russell as the headline stars for a very special event being held in Paris in ten days!"

"A fashion show?" Blythe was so excited her voice sounded all squeaky.

"Better," Mona declared. "A fashion show at the first-ever

Everyday Hero Awards, on the runway at Paris airport!"

"Mona, I'm honoured," Blythe said.

"Yes, of course you are," Mona replied. "All eyes will be on you!"

Blythe grabbed her notebook and a pen. "Which fashions should I bring for the show?" she asked.

"Bring? No, no, no – you mean design," Mona corrected her. "We want all-new designs to make their debut here, Blythe. I want you to think daring and dramatic for your designs. Just like the heroes we'll be honouring."

"I'm sorry – did you say all-new designs?" she repeated. "For a show that's in two weeks?"

"Not two weeks. Ten days," Mona said. "I'm sure you can come up with at least seven new designs by then."

"Um, yes, of course," Blythe said. But inside, she was about ten seconds away from panicking! Mona was asking for a lot.

"Since you'll be the only designer for this show, you'll make all the big decisions – from sets and lights, to models—"

"You mean I can choose the pet models, all by myself?"

"Exactly," replied Mona. "I'll call back soon to finalise all the details. Be ready to wow me, Blythe! Ciao!"

And just like that, Blythe's phone went silent.

"Bye, Mona," Blythe whispered. She had an international fashion show to prepare for.

There wasn't a moment to lose!

Chapter 2
The Perfect Poster

The next morning, Blythe's dad, Roger, put on his pilot uniform and went to the kitchen to make some coffee. He was surprised to see that Blythe was already there.

"What day is it?" Roger asked. "I could've sworn it was Saturday—"

"It *is* Saturday, Dad," Blythe replied. "You are never going to believe the phone call I got!" She quickly told him everything.

"I know it's pretty last minute, but can you take the pets and me to Paris in ten days?" Blythe asked.

"Are you kidding?" Roger exclaimed. "It will be an honour to fly you to Paris!"

"Thank you so much!" Though she missed him when he had to travel for work, there were a lot of perks to having a pilot for a father. And with the fully equipped Pet Jet at their service, Blythe and her pals from the Littlest Pet Shop could always travel in style.

"I can't wait to tell the pets about the trip! I know they'll be so excited—"

Too late Blythe realised what she'd said. "I mean, their owners will be so excited," she quickly corrected herself. Not even Blythe's dad knew that she could communicate with animals. Luckily, though, he didn't seem to notice her slip.

"That's my girl," said Roger.

"I guess I'll head downstairs," she said. "Mrs Twombly should be opening the shop any minute now."

When Blythe arrived at the Littlest Pet Shop and told the owner, Mrs Twombly, all about Mona Autumn's phone call, Mrs Twombly's mouth dropped open. "Oh, Blythe! I'm so happy for you!" she squealed.

"I still can't believe it,"

replied Blythe. "If you'll excuse me, I need to go and see how my models are doing today!"

Blythe pushed through the curtain that separated the shop from the Day Camp. All the regulars had arrived.

"Guess what, everybody?" Blythe asked. "Mona Autumn called with big news!"

A Cavalier King Charles spaniel named Zoe pranced right over. Modelling Blythe's fabulous fashions was one of Zoe's favourite things to do … so when Zoe heard the name "Mona Autumn", she couldn't wait to find out more.

Blythe took a deep breath as the rest of the pets gathered around her. "The latest issue of *Tres Blasé* has had record-breaking sales, so Mona has invited me to do a special fashion show at an awards ceremony … in Paris! And here's the best part – since the show is going to feature my designs exclusively, I get to choose all the models. That means that all of you can be in the show!"

"Oh, Blythe," Zoe cried, fluttering her long eyelashes. "I've always wanted to star in a fashion show in the fashion capital of the world!"

Blythe tried to hide her smile. "Well, you'll all be stars," Blythe explained.

"So when is this show?" Russell asked.

"Well …" Blythe began, biting her lip a little. "It's in ten days – so we have our work cut out for us."

"Don't you worry, Blythe," Zoe said confidently. "I have complete faith in you!"

"Thanks, Zoe," Blythe said. "I guess I just—"

Bzzzz!

Blythe's phone was buzzing again. "Maybe it's Mona Autumn!" she exclaimed. At the same time, the Littlest Pet Shop phone started ringing, too.

"Anyway, I just need to – " Blythe continued, as she searched for her phone.

Bzzzz! Brrring!

" – stay – "

Bzzzz! Brrring!

" – focused!" Blythe finished triumphantly as she finally found her phone at the bottom of her bag. "Hello? Oh, hi, Youngmee."

Youngmee Song worked at the Sweet Delights Sweet Shoppe next door.

"Look outside?" Blythe said, confused. "Why? Oh … OK. Call you right back."

Blythe hung up and turned back to the pets. "Youngmee's being very mysterious," she said. "We'd better see what's up."

The pets followed Blythe to the front of the shop, where Mrs Twombly was frantically trying to handle the phone. The instant she finished one call, the phone started ringing again! Beyond that, though, the shop was packed with customers. Blythe couldn't remember a time when so many people had packed into the small shop.

There was no doubt about it: something very unusual was happening.

Chapter 3
Stars on Set

Blythe crossed the shop and opened
the door. Her mouth dropped open.
The pavement in front of the Littlest Pet
Shop was crowded with photographers,
reporters and cameramen.

That was when the reporters noticed
her. "Blythe!" they cried, as they rushed

over. "Just a few questions – a quick interview—"

Quick-thinking Minka darted around Blythe and slammed the door shut. Blythe grabbed the remote control from the counter  and turned on the TV – just in time to catch a glimpse of herself standing in the doorway of the Littlest Pet Shop as Minka slammed the door!

"That's – here?" Blythe asked in shock.

"Shhh!" Vinnie said, as the reporter started talking – but to Mrs Twombly and all the customers, it sounded like an ordinary gecko noise.

"Blythe Baxter, chief designer of the Blythe Style line of pet fashions, has been handpicked by fashion pioneer Mona Autumn as the featured designer for an upcoming show in Paris!" the reporter said into her microphone.

Blythe stood there in shock, and her phone slid from her hand.

"The Paris offices of *Tres Blasé* have announced that more details will be released soon," the reporter continued breathlessly. "Until then, we suggest you snatch up as many Blythe Style original pet fashions as you can!"

At that moment, someone in the shop glanced up at the TV just as Blythe's school picture came on the screen. The customer's gaze drifted over to Blythe.

"Blythe?" she shrieked. "*The* Blythe Baxter of Blythe Style? Can I get your autograph?"

"Me too!" another woman exclaimed.

"And one for my daughter? And my niece? And my next-door neighbour's second cousin?"

"Uh...uh...uh..." Blythe stammered, as the crowd surged around her.

Luckily, the pets knew just what to do. They surrounded Blythe and quickly nudged her towards the Day Camp area of the shop, where customers weren't allowed.

"Thanks, everybody," she said gratefully. "That was..."

"Intense," suggested Sunil.

"Insane," Russell said, shaking his head.

"Incredible!" Zoe added. "Blythe, can you believe it? You're an international superstar!"

But a worried expression settled over Blythe's face. "It's kind of overwhelming," she confessed. "All those people acting like I'm a celebrity…"

"Look at it this way," Pepper pointed out. "Mrs Twombly is now going to sell even more stuff than usual… All thanks to you!"

"It's just quite a lot of pressure," Blythe said. "What if I can't get everything done in time?"

Russell knew that he had to find a way to reassure Blythe. "You know," he began, "I just had an idea. Why don't we focus on plans for the fashion show itself… while you focus on the new designs?"

"You'd do that for me?" she asked.

"Of course we would," Russell assured her. "You'll still be in charge, of course," Russell continued. "Nobody does fashion like you do! But we can do a lot of the planning work for you behind the scenes."

"I don't know what to say," Blythe told them. "It would actually make the fashion show feel like fun again!"

"And it should be fun," Russell said firmly. "Don't worry about the runway; focus on the FUN-way! Project FUN-way! So, what do you say?"

"Yes – a million times over!" Blythe replied at once.

Russell grinned as he whipped out a notebook and pencil. "Let's get started right away! What do you think the feel of the show should be?"

"Daring and dramatic," Blythe said.

"Let us worry about that," Russell told her. "Why don't you get to work on your designs, and we'll have a meeting later this afternoon to see what everyone's come up with."

"That sounds perfect," Blythe said. "If you need anything at all, you know where to find me."

Blythe hurried off to the side room where she stored all her sewing supplies. Russell turned to the pets and held his arms open wide. "For starters, I don't think we should interrupt Blythe for any reason at all," he said.

"I agree," said Penny. "Besides, no matter what comes up, we can handle it."

"That's the right attitude!" Russell said approvingly.

"I'm so glad you're going to be in charge, Russell," said Minka, as she hopped from one foot to the other. "You're the most organised hedgehog I know!"

"Me? In charge?" Russell asked in surprise. "No, no, that's not what I meant at all. I was just—"

"But somebody's got to be in charge," Pepper interrupted him. "Otherwise, we won't know who's doing what."

"They're right, buddy," Vinnie spoke up. "You're the perfect hedgehog for the job."

"Well…if you're all sure," Russell said as he finally gave in. "I'll only be in charge if everybody wants me to be in charge. Let's have a vote!"

Russell made sure that the tip of his pencil was extra sharp as he wrote everyone's names down in his notebook. "Everybody who thinks that I should be in charge, please raise your paw," he said in a very serious-sounding voice.

In an instant, Minka's, Pepper's, Penny Ling's, Sunil's and Vinnie's paws shot into the air. Russell blushed with happiness as he made a check mark next to each name. The vote was almost unanimous…almost.

Russell's smile faded. "Where's Zoe?" he asked.

The other pets looked around the room. Somehow, Zoe had slipped away from the group.

"Hmm," Russell said. "I guess our first

order of business will be...finding Zoe. It's pretty clear that she's not in the Day Camp area. Which can only mean..."

As Russell's voice trailed off, everyone looked toward the shop section of the Littlest Pet Shop.

"Remember, we can't bother Blythe," Russell told his friends. "You stay here. I'm going in."

Russell crept towards the shop, wondering what he'd find there.

Nothing could have prepared him for the reality: Zoe was strutting back and forth on the counter, modelling Blythe's creations as all the photographers took pictures of her!

A wide grin crossed Russell's face. The call of the cameras and the lure of the spotlight were just too tempting for Zoe to resist. But how would he ever convince her to come back to Day Camp?

Maybe I don't have to bring Zoe back with me, he thought. *Her modelling is boosting sales ... and she's keeping the photographers busy, which means they're not bugging Blythe. Yes!*

Russell couldn't have been more pleased with his first decision as leader. If everything else went this smoothly, Russell was confident that pulling off the fashion show would be a piece of cake!

Chapter 4
Friends Reunited

Over the next few days, Russell worked
nonstop to come up with ideas for
Project Funway. Eventually, his notebook
was full of them — a huge white tent,
extra-bright clear light bulbs, silver
sawhorses. *This might actually work,*
Russell thought excitedly. *By keeping*

everything in the background as plain as possible, Blythe's fashions will really pop!

"Russell!" Zoe gushed, as she hurried up to him. "I was thinking...how can we make a fashion show even more dramatic and exciting? And you know what I thought of? Circuses!"

"Circuses?" he repeated.

"Yes, exactly!" Zoe said. "Lion tamers... trapeze artists...high-wire acts...you just don't get more dramatic than that!"

"I...guess not," Russell said. He didn't want to hurt Zoe's feelings. But the truth was, Russell thought her idea was all wrong!

Zoe clapped her paws together. "Oh, I just knew you'd agree!" she cried. "Now, here's what we'll need."

Slowly, Russell reached for his notebook. *I guess it wouldn't hurt to* write it down, he thought. *It will make Zoe feel like she's an important part of our team. And I'll just make sure that my ideas are the ones we use in the show.*

"For starters, we need giant spotlights in all colours," Zoe said excitedly. "And… some kind of fancy tinsel curtain for the backdrop. And you know what would be really great?"

"What?" Russell asked hesitantly. He didn't know how much more "greatness" he could handle!

"We could hire trapeze artists to perform in the air while we're all walking the runway!" Zoe exclaimed.

"Right. Trapeze artists," Russell said, but this time didn't even write it down.

"Aren't you going to add it to the list?" she asked.

"Oh. Sure, I guess," Russell said.

Minka scampered over to them. "Hey! What are you guys doing?" she asked.

"I was just telling Russell all about my vision for Blythe's show," Zoe told her.

"Ooh, you know what? I had an idea for the show, too!" Minka exclaimed.

Russell brightened a little. Everyone knew that Minka was incredibly artistic.

"Fireballs!" Minka announced.

"Fireballs?" Russell and Zoe repeated in disbelief. Russell was relieved to see that Zoe looked as shocked as he felt.

"Special effects. Pyro-what's-it-called," Minka continued.

"Minka, you're a genius!" Zoe declared.

Russell shook his head. *Did I hear Zoe correctly?* he wondered. *Surely she didn't just say that Minka's—*

"An absolute genius!" Zoe continued. "Fireballs are perfect. Talk about danger! Real fire and flames lighting up the runway! In fact—"

"Whoa," Russell interrupted. "That's way too dangerous!"

Minka scrunched up her face. "But, Russell, the theme of the show is danger," she pointed out. "Dangerous and dramatic."

"No!" Russell yelped, shaking his head. "First, it's *daring* and dramatic. Not dangerous and dramatic. And second – no fire at all!"

"But I know for a fact that Blythe has been working on a firefighter-inspired fashion design," Zoe said. "Not to mention, fire fits in perfectly with my circus theme!"

Russell knew he had to put a stop to this crazy idea before it went any further. He took a deep breath and said, as calmly as he could, "I agree that it sounds very exciting and dramatic. But the truth is, real fire is just too dangerous for my fashion show."

"*Your* fashion show?" Zoe repeated. "I thought it was Blythe's fashion show."

Every last one of Russell's prickly spines bristled. "Yes, and everyone voted for me to be in charge," he snapped.

Minka and Zoe exchanged a worried look.

"But Blythe would still want to hear all

our ideas," Minka
pointed out.

"I agree," Zoe said.
"Add Minka's idea
to the list. If Blythe
doesn't want to do it,
then that's her decision."

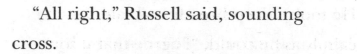

"All right," Russell said, sounding
cross.

Zoe and Minka watched as Russell
scribbled the word "fireballs" on the list.
"Thanks, Russell," Minka said in a quiet
voice. She almost sounded sad. "I...only
wanted to help."

"You know, Minka, if you really want to
help – help Blythe!" Russell suggested.

"Help Blythe? How?" she asked. "I
thought I was helping by staying out of
her way."

"Minka, from now on, it's your job to

be at Blythe's beck and call! It's up to you to figure out what Blythe needs – even before she knows she needs it!"

Minka looked baffled. "How in the world am I supposed to do that?" she asked.

"Never leave her side," Russell ordered. "If she takes her last sip of water, you get her a new water bottle before she has a chance to ask for one. If she finishes her snack—"

"Get her another one," Minka finished for him.

"Yes!" Russell exclaimed. "You know, it's a big job. So, Zoe, you'd better help, too."

"Well, sure, I guess," Zoe replied.

"You know," Russell said, "she might need

something right now – and there's no one there to help her!"

"I guess we'd better hurry, then!" Minka said.

As Minka and Zoe hurried off to Blythe's sewing room at the back of the shop, Russell sighed with relief. *Now I can get back to plans for Project Funway without any more silly interruptions.*

Even as the thought crossed his mind, Russell's spines prickled a little. He knew that Zoe and Minka weren't silly interruptions. But Russell pushed the thought from his mind. Right now, he had to focus on Project Funway.

No matter what.

Chapter 5

Stress in the Shop!

When Blythe finally finished sewing the last stitch on the last outfit, the sudden silence of her sewing machine filled the entire Day Camp.

"I'm done," Blythe said, looking tired but happy.

A tremendous cheer arose from all the

pets as they swarmed around Blythe to congratulate her.

"We knew you could do it, Blythe!" Zoe said. "No one has more talent than you!"

"Or works harder," Russell added.

The pets could tell how happy Russell's and Zoe's compliments made Blythe – even if she blushed a little.

"Three cheers for Blythe!" continued Russell.

As the pets began cheering again, Zoe and Minka exchanged a relieved glance. For the first time in days, Russell seemed like his old self again: supportive, friendly and, most of all, fun.

"Thanks, everybody!" Blythe replied. "There's no way I would've got it done without you."

Blythe knelt down so that she and Russell were face to face. "And how can I ever thank you for everything you've done?" she asked him. "Knowing that you were taking care of all the details for the show let me focus on creating all the new outfits."

Russell puffed up with pride. "Well, you know," he said, "whatever it takes to make Project Funway a success! So... when can we see your new creations?"

Blythe pretended to check her watch. "I don't know," she said playfully. "How about...right now!"

"This way," Russell said, as he herded the pets to one side. "Make room for Blythe! Don't crowd her! Move along!"

A funny expression crossed Blythe's face. She'd never heard Russell talk like that – especially not to the other pets at Day Camp. "No, it's OK," she said lightly. "I'll be right back with my new designs."

Blythe returned, pushing a rolling clothing rack alongside her. "I present Blythe Style's newest collection – Courage Couture!" she announced proudly.

As everyone rushed over to examine each outfit, Russell realised this was the perfect opportunity to talk to Blythe alone. "Blythe, do you have a minute to talk about plans for Project Funway?" he asked in a low voice.

"Sure," replied Blythe.

Russell beckoned for Blythe to follow him to the opposite end of Day Camp. "Everyone's had a lot of…ideas," he began. Then he paused as Blythe yawned suddenly.

"Sorry," she apologised. "I haven't been getting enough sleep lately. Go on."

"As I was saying, everyone's had a lot of ideas. Some good…and some terrible," Russell explained.

Blythe looked surprised. "Terrible?" she repeated. Had Russell really said something so harsh?

"Terrible," Russell repeated. "You'll see for yourself. I've written them all down in my notebook. I didn't want to hurt anyone's feelings. But there is absolutely no way they should be part of Project Funway!"

Blythe frowned. "But, Russell," she said,

"don't you think that everyone should be able to contribute?"

Russell made a face. "Project Funway is too important. Trust me! I'm in charge, and I take that very seriously!"

Blythe wasn't sure how to respond. She truly believed that everyone's ideas were important. But on the other hand, she knew how hard Russell had been working to organise every last detail.

Russell pressed his notebook into her hands. "Here are all the notes and requirements for the show," he explained. "If there's an "X" next to it, email it to Mona Autumn's people in Paris so that they can take care of the arrangements. But if there's a star next to it, just ignore it."

"X – email. Star – ignore," Blythe repeated. "I'll send this first thing tomorrow. I'm going to go home and go to bed early."

"No! Blythe, you've got to send it tonight!" he exclaimed. "It's six hours later in Paris…so if you send it tonight, the team can get right to work tomorrow morning. Otherwise, they might not have a chance to get started until tomorrow night, or the next day, which is really the day after tomorrow, or otherwise known as next Tuesday, which might not—"

Blythe held up her hands. "OK, I'll

send it tonight," she said.

After she said goodbye to the pets and to Mrs Twombly, Blythe sneaked out of the back entrance to avoid being mobbed by all her brand-new fans!

"Hey, here's my favourite internationally famous fashion designer!" Roger announced with a grin, as she walked in the door. From the smell of garlic and tomatoes in the air, Blythe could tell he was making spaghetti and meatballs. "Hope you're hungry!"

"It smells great, Dad," Blythe said, with another yawn.

Roger stirred the sauce. Then he took a tiny taste. "Mmm, perfect!" he announced. "We'll eat in five minutes. Would you set the table, please?"

Blythe paused. *I guess the email can wait a little while,* she finally decided. *Besides, I am pretty hungry.*

As soon as dinner was over, Blythe helped clear the table and do the dishes. Then she went to her bedroom. While she waited for her email to load, Blythe opened Russell's notebook.

Blythe scrunched up her face as she flipped through the pages. He'd made notes about everything – from the theme and the backdrop to the travel arrangements and the lighting!

This almost seems like too much, Blythe thought.

Blythe shook her head. *Russell knows what he's doing,* she reminded herself. *I'll just have to figure out the right way to ask for all these requests. But first, I have to figure out which ones Russell wanted me to send.*

It wasn't easy to tell which marks were Xs and which were stars. All the smudgy, scraggly marks Russell had made looked pretty similar.

Those are probably the stars, Blythe finally decided. She started typing an email to one of Mona Autumn's assistants.

Bonjour, Marie!

I am so excited to send these requests for the fashion show. I know this list is long, so if any of our requests are too difficult, feel free to change them for something easier. The new outfits are finished, too – so we're just about ready to leave! Thank you for everything, Marie – or should I say, merci beaucoup?

XOXO,

Blythe

Then Blythe typed up the long list of
notes Russell had made, from sparkly
tinsel curtains and spotlights in every
colour to trapeze artists and fireballs!
There was no doubt in her mind that
Project Funway was going to be exciting!

Chapter 6
A Head for Heights

Just twenty-four hours later, Blythe and the pets boarded the Pet Jet and settled in for an overnight flight to Paris.

"Attention, this is your captain speaking." Roger's voice crackled over the speakers. "Please prepare for takeoff."

The plane's door closed and locked with a loud whoosh. Blythe glanced around the jet. "Is everybody's seatbelt buckled?" she asked, as she did a quick head count. "Wait a second – I only see six seats filled. Who's missing?"

"I'm here," Zoe called.

"Me too," added Sunil.

"And me three!" Vinnie piped up.

"There's Pepper, Penny and Minka," Blythe said, as she counted the others. "Which means…Russell's not here!"

Blythe scrambled out of her seat and sprinted over to the intercom. "Dad!" she said urgently. "Don't leave yet."

"What's the problem?" Roger replied.

"Russell's not here," Blythe explained. "Let me—"

Suddenly, Zoe hopped onto the armrest of her seat. "I see him!" she shrieked. "Russell's still on the runway!"

"What!" Blythe cried. She rushed over and looked out of the window. Sure enough, the hedgehog was perched on a baggage cart.

Blythe went back to the intercom. "It's OK, Dad – we found him," she reported. "But Russell's still out on the tarmac! Can you open the door again?"

"I'll open the door now," Mr Baxter said, "but be careful on the tarmac, Blythe."

As soon as the door opened, Blythe hurried down the steps.

She swooped down and gathered Russell into her arms. "Russell!" she hissed. "What were you thinking?"

"Oh, hi, Blythe," Russell replied. "What's the matter?"

"What's the matter?" she repeated in disbelief. "We could've left without you – that's what's the matter! Why are you still on the tarmac when everyone else is ready for take off?"

"Well, somebody had to make sure that all the luggage was properly loaded," Russell explained calmly.

"The baggage handlers know what they're doing," Blythe retorted.

"No way, Blythe," Russell said. "I'm in charge, and I—"

"—take that very seriously," Blythe

finished for him, with a sigh.

As soon as they were on board the Pet Jet, Blythe told her father that they were ready for take off. A giant grin crossed Blythe's face as she stared out of the window. No matter how many times Blythe flew somewhere on the Pet Jet, she always loved the swoopy thrill she felt when the plane took off.

Zoe pushed a button to make her seat recline. "Time for a little beauty rest," she announced. "But, don't worry, I made sure my owners packed my Blythe Style sleep mask and my Blythe Style earmuffs in my carry-on bag."

"Hey, look!" Vinnie yelled excitedly. "They're showing *Space Lizards: Race Against Time* tonight."

"Ahem." Russell cleared his throat to get everyone's attention. But the other pets were chattering so much that no one noticed.

"Blythe, would you paint my nails?" Penny Ling asked.

"Sure," replied Blythe. "What colour do you want?"

"Ahem!" Russell said again, louder this time.

"Ooh, mine too!" Pepper spoke up.

"AHEM!" Russell shouted at the top of his lungs. "These are all very good plans … for the flight home. But, for now, we've got work to do!"

"What do you mean?" Blythe asked in confusion. "Everything's packed and loaded…"

"We never practised," Russell explained. "You know, all those important fashion show moves."

"Oh," Blythe replied. "I'm sure we'll have time tomorrow for a quick run-through."

"What if we don't?" Russell argued. "To be honest, I'm surprised by your attitude. I'd think that you of all people would care about the show as much as I do!"

"Of course I care about the show," Blythe said, stung. "But I also care about everybody getting the chance to take a break and...relax."

"We can relax when the show is over," Russell said firmly. "But as soon as Blythe's dad turns off the fasten-seatbelt sign—"

Ding!

Everyone looked up as the seatbelt sign suddenly went dark. Russell clapped his paws together. "Everybody up!" he announced.

Blythe tried not to sigh as the pets slowly unbuckled their seat belts and joined Russell in the aisle – all except Zoe. With her sleep mask and earmuffs, she'd missed the entire conversation!

"You too, Zoe," Russell called. But Zoe still snoozed, entirely oblivious until Russell marched right over to her and snapped the sleep mask off her head!

"Huh…what…hey!" Zoe yelped.

"Sorry to wake you, Zoe, but we've got a lot of practising to do," Russell told her.

"You woke me up to practise? I've modelled in pet shows all over the world! I'll be fine tomorrow."

"Oh, I'm sure that *you* can handle it, Zoe," Russell said in a quiet voice. "But… can they?"

He pointed over to the aisle, where Vinnie and Sunil had already started practising their best modelling moves – with hilariously awful results!

"Hmm," Zoe replied. "I see what you mean."

"I know we can get everyone ready by the time this plane lands," Russell declared.

"I don't know, Russell," Blythe said. "A good night's sleep might be just as useful as a whole night of practice."

"There will be plenty of time to relax and have fun at the after-party, Blythe," Russell said firmly. "OK! When I call your name, I want you to walk down the aisle just like you would during the show. Vinnie! You're up!"

Blythe settled into one of the seats, but she didn't look happy about it.

And neither did the pets.

Chapter 7
It Takes Two!

Eight hours later, the Pet Jet finally landed. Russell was pleased with the pets' modelling moves. But he was the only one with a smile on his face. Everyone else was tired, grumpy and ready for a long nap.

"Look over there," Blythe said,

pointing through the window. "It's our hotel. In the airport! So we'll be able to check in as soon as we get off the plane."

"Not so fast, Blythe," Russell said. "We have to make sure everything's ready for the show."

"No, Russell. Everyone needs to rest," Blythe argued. "Remember, this is Project FUN-way."

"Blythe," Zoe spoke up suddenly. "It looks like there are some people here to see you."

Blythe turned in her seat to glance through Zoe's window. Sure enough, a group of *Tres Blasé* staffers were waiting on the tarmac.

"Check out that purple tent over there – I bet that's where they're holding Project Funway!" Blythe exclaimed.

"A purple tent?" Russell asked,

sounding confused. "I specifically said a silver tent. And if the tent's wrong, maybe the lights are wrong. And if the lights are wrong, maybe the backdrop's wrong. And if—"

"*Tres Blasé* is a huge international magazine," Blythe told him. "I'm sure they know what they're doing."

"Well, I can tell you one thing," Russell said stubbornly. "I am not going to the hotel until I personally check all the preparations for the show. Sometimes I think that I'm the only one who cares about Project Funway!"

Zoe couldn't take any more of Russell's attitude. "Listen up!" she said hotly. But before

she could continue, Blythe placed a calming hand on Zoe's back.

"I know this has been really hard," Blythe whispered close to Zoe's ear. "But I'm sure Russell will be back to his usual self as soon as the show gets underway. We'll get some rest and, before you know it, we'll be walking down the catwalk at Project Funway, and all of this will feel so silly and trivial!"

A small smile flickered across Zoe's face. "It will be amazing, won't it?"

"Come on!" Blythe replied, as the plane finally came to a stop. "Let's go and greet our friends from *Tres Blasé!*"

Blythe and her dad were the first ones

to exit the plane, with the pets filing behind them in a row.

"Blythe! Darling! So good to see you again," gushed Mona Autumn. "And are these all your little models? How adorable!"

"Allow me to introduce Zoe, Pepper, Penny Ling, Minka, Vinnie and Sunil. And I'm sure you remember…Russell? Has anyone seen Russell?" Blythe said.

All eyes turned towards the purple tent, where they could see Russell's prickly silhouette. No one spoke as he turned around and scurried over to the group.

"WRONG!" he howled. "It's – all – WRONG!"

To Blythe and the pets, every angry word coming out of Russell's mouth was crystal clear. But to

everyone else on the tarmac, all they saw was a furious little hedgehog, chattering and squeaking frantically as he jumped up and down.

"This is totally dreadful!" Zoe growled under her breath. "Russell is making a fool of us in front of the entire staff of *Tres Blasé!*"

"I know exactly what this situation needs," Vinnie announced loudly. "A distraction!"

"I said velvet curtains! *Velvet!*" Russell wailed.

Just then, Vinnie leaped off the ground and sailed over Russell's head. In mid-air, he struck his best pose from the all-night practice session. Some of the staffers gasped…but they started giggling again when Vinnie crashed into the baggage cart.

"That was...unexpected," Mona Autumn said.

"I, um, I can explain," Blythe said helplessly.

"And those lights! I was very clear about the lights! All white spotlights! None of this rainbow-light nonsense!" Russell yelled.

"Blythe," Mona said, "is he quite all right? Should I call a vet?"

"He's fine," Blythe said shortly. Then she buried her head in her hands. Zoe was right – this was a disaster. "Russell," Blythe said firmly. She knelt down so that she and Russell could see eye to eye. "RUSSELL!"

At last, Blythe had Russell's attention.

"This has gone too far," Blythe said.

"You can't treat your friends like this."

"Blythe! They've gone and done the exact opposite of everything I planned for the show!" he howled in response. "All those terrible ideas from everybody else—"

"Terrible ideas?" Zoe asked. But Blythe held up a finger.

Russell's eyes grew wide. "How did the people at *Tres Blasé* even know about everybody else's ideas?"

Blythe thought back to the night when she'd emailed Marie. She remembered how she hadn't been quite sure which marks were stars and which marks were Xs...

"I, uh...I may have sent the wrong list," she admitted. "I'm sorry. It was an accident. But Project Funway is still going to be amazing! We're all together in Paris

– the fashion capital of the world! It's fantastic, isn't it?"

Russell stared at the ground for a long moment. "Yeah. I guess," he said. "But can't you tell Mona there was a terrible mistake, and we really need to get my silver sawhorses instead, and—"

"No, Russell," she said gently. "Let's check into the hotel. Everything will look better after a big breakfast and a little rest."

"Maybe," Russell replied – but he didn't sound convinced. All his spines prickled with unhappiness as he watched everyone line up for the tram.

Chapter 8
The Dress Rehearsal

There was so much commotion as everyone prepared to board the tram that no one noticed as Russell took one last, wistful glance at the purple tent.

How can Project Funway go on without the right kind of tent? Or the perfect lights? he thought sadly.

It felt like everything was going to be ruined.

Maybe it's not too late, Russell thought suddenly. *If I skipped the hotel and went into the city instead…maybe I could find just what we need to make the show perfect after all.*

In an instant, Russell made up his mind. He scurried in the opposite direction and leaped onto the luggage cart. Russell waited – hardly daring to breathe – for someone to notice he was missing.

But in all the commotion, no one did.

When the luggage cart lurched forward, Russell breathed a sigh of relief. He was on his way to save the show!

There was so much hustle and bustle at the airport that no one paid much attention to Russell at all – not even

when he hitched a ride on a rolling suitcase and sneaked into the back of a taxi that took him straight to the heart of Paris!

Standing on the cobblestone street, Russell took a deep breath. The entire city seemed magical – like a place where anything could happen. *I want to see everything!* he thought excitedly. *I wish everybody else was here, too. I wish we could all explore Paris together.*

Russell shook his head. *Focus, Russell!*

he scolded himself. *It's up to you to save Project Funway and make it as amazing as you know it can be!*

Russell tried to figure out what he needed first. That's when he realised something: his important notebook, filled with every single idea he'd had for Project Funway, was still in Blythe's carry-on bag!

"Arrgghh!" Without his notebook, he'd have to try to remember every single thing he wanted to have at the show. But that was hundreds of items! *Those exposed clear light bulbs,* he thought suddenly. *Lighting is a really big deal at a fashion show. And the silver sawhorses…I could probably find some regular ones and paint them silver…but then I'd also need silver paint…and will the paint even dry in time for the show? Minka would* know! I wish she was here!

Russell sighed. *One thing at a time,* he told himself. *Light bulbs first!*

But Paris was an enormous city... and Russell didn't know how to find anything. The shops on this particular street sold gorgeous dresses, fancy shoes and expensive perfumes. *Wow, Blythe and Zoe have got to see this!* Russell thought excitedly as he peeked into one shop. But his smile faded when he remembered that his friends were all back at the hotel.

Russell checked shop after shop, but none of them sold light bulbs, let alone sawhorses or silver paint.

No big deal, Russell thought. *I bet they'll be selling something I need on the next street...or the one just beyond that...*

But even though Russell roamed the streets of Paris for hours, he never found what he was looking for. It would've been easier if Pepper had been there to make him laugh. *Or Penny,* Russell thought sadly. *Somehow, Penny always knows just what to say when I'm feeling bad about something.*

After Russell had hitched a ride on a bus, he arrived in a completely different section of the city. Now Russell was surrounded by sleek, glittering skyscrapers that reached high into the sky. *Where am I?* he wondered.

Surrounded by people hurrying past him on the pavement, Russell suddenly felt all alone in the world.

Chapter 9
Wake-up Call

A few hours later, Blythe awoke in an enormous bed. It took her half a second to remember where she was: a hotel in Paris, on the day of the Project Funway fashion show!

In an instant, Blythe was out of bed and on her feet. "Guys!" she cried excitedly.

"Wake up! Project Funway starts in two hours!"

From cosy pet beds scattered around the room, all the pets awoke. Just like Blythe, their jet lag immediately transformed into excitement.

Blythe's phone started buzzing. "I just got a text from Mona," she announced. "It's just about time to start getting ready!"

"So…" Penny began, sounding a little uncertain. "Should we change into our outfits here?"

"Yeah," added Pepper. "What happens next?"

Zoe immediately took charge. "Not to worry, darlings, you're working with a seasoned professional," she assured them. "We'll

go right over to that great big tent on the tarmac. There will be a special VIP-only section, just for us. That stands for Very Important Pets, you know."

Vinnie's eyes lit up. "Very Important Pets? I could get used to that!" he said.

"It's going to be fabulous," Zoe assured him. "The best grooming you've ever had in your entire life! And then, once everybody's ready, we'll change into Blythe's wonderful outfits and get ready to show the world just what Blythe can do!"

"Thanks, Zoe," Blythe said. "And on that note, we'll do one last wardrobe check before we head down to the tent!"

Blythe crossed the room to the rolling rack where she had carefully hung each outfit before collapsing into bed. "Let's see," she began. "Zoe...Penny...Sunil...

Vinnie…Minka…Pepper…Russell…"

One by one, each pet stepped forward to take the outfit from Blythe – except for Russell.

Blythe glanced around the room. "Has anyone seen Russell?"

"Actually, now that you mention it… no," Zoe said.

"Well, he's gotta be here somewhere!" Pepper announced, poking her head under the bed.

"He's not on the balcony," Sunil reported.

"He's not in the bathroom, either," added Vinnie.

"Has anyone seen him since we were on the tarmac?" Blythe asked urgently.

Silence fell over the room as all the

pets tried to remember the last time they'd seen Russell. In the long pause that followed, it was obvious that no one had seen Russell since his tantrum.

Blythe swallowed hard. "I thought we all checked into the hotel together. But – how – oh, I feel just terrible!"

Zoe rushed over to her. "Now, now, Blythe, you can't blame yourself," she said soothingly. "It's been absolutely crazy-busy and exhausting."

"Yeah," Vinnie chimed in. "What we have to do now is figure out where Russell went."

"Well…he was really upset about the arrangements for the show," Blythe said thoughtfully. "There was that big mix-up, and…I think…Russell was determined to make his vision for Project Funway happen… But – that would mean—"

"Going shopping in Paris – all by himself!" cried Zoe.

"It's not the shopping I'm worried about," Blythe said. "It's Russell, all by himself in a strange, big city... Well, as they say, the show must go on. But not without Russell. We've got to figure out a way to bring him back!"

"How would we get into the city?" asked Minka. "Call a taxi?"

"I have another idea," Blythe said as she grabbed her phone. "Hello? Dad? We have an emergency! Russell is missing... I think he's in the city... Yes! That's exactly what I was thinking!"

When Blythe turned back to the pets, her eyes were shining with hope. "Dad's going to get permission to fly over Paris in one of the airport's helicopters," she said breathlessly. "With a bird's-eye view, I'm sure we can spot Russell!"

"Hooray!" all the pets cheered.

"Come on," Blythe said. "Let's change into our outfits here, tell Mona Autumn everything, and then hit the skies!"

Moments later, Blythe dashed out of the hotel room in her search-and-rescue uniform, with all the pets scurrying behind her. They found Mona Autumn in the middle of the tent, barking orders into her headset.

"We have a problem," Blythe said in a rush. "One of my models is missing, and the show can't start without him."

"That's not a problem," Mona said in an airy voice. "Models can easily be replaced."

"Not Russell the hedgehog," Blythe said firmly. "Because he isn't just one of my models...he's one of my friends."

For the first time, Blythe truly had Mona's attention. "The hedgehog? But he's a fan favourite! Enormously popular! Don't tell me he got cold paws!"

"No...I think there's something else going on," Blythe replied.

"Just like there would be no show without Blythe, I don't see how we can have a show without Russell," Mona announced.

"We have a plan to find him," Blythe spoke up. "My dad's going to fly us over

Paris in a helicopter."

"All right," Mona agreed. "Good idea. But you're taking one of my photographers with you. If the show can't go on, at least we'll have some high-action shots of your adventures for the next issue of *Tres Blasé*."

"Fine! Absolutely!" Blythe exclaimed. Then she turned to the pets. "Come on, everybody! Let's go!"

Across the tarmac, Roger was testing the controls of the helicopter. Blythe helped all the pets board the chopper before she climbed on, too.

"Ready to go?" Roger asked.

Just then, a man carrying an expensive camera approached the helicopter. "My name is Marc," he said, with just the hint of a French accent. "Is this the search-and-rescue mission for the model?"

"It's a search-and-rescue mission for our friend," Blythe corrected him. "Hurry. We're about to take off."

The moment Roger was cleared for takeoff, he piloted the helicopter into the sky.

Blythe craned her neck as she glanced out of the window at the glittering city. From up in the sky, Paris seemed bigger than ever.

How in the world were they going to find one little hedgehog among all the world-famous landmarks, buildings, people and pets?

Chapter 10
Time to Shine!

Meanwhile, in the heart of Paris, the loneliness inside Russell got worse with every passing moment. He didn't know what to do or where to go – but he was certain about one thing: figuring things out would've been a lot easier with his pals by his side.

I need them, he realised suddenly. *I need them a whole lot more than I need special light bulbs or silver paint…or anything else in the world.*

Just like that, Russell realised how wrong he'd been about Project Funway. Somehow, in his eagerness to make everything perfect, he'd forgotten about the fun part… and he'd forgotten about his friends' feelings, too.

Blythe was right, he thought. *None of that other stuff matters! And if I don't get back to the airport soon, I'm going to miss the show!*

With his mind made up and his heart full of determination, Russell charged forward.

Then he stopped.

Where is the airport? he wondered.

Surrounded by towering skyscrapers

that blocked his view in every direction, Russell couldn't tell.

Now Russell was really worried. *If I can't find the airport, I can't get back to my friends,* he thought anxiously, as he started pacing back and forth.

"*Pardonnez-moi!*" a voice said, as Russell suddenly collided with someone!

"Ow!" Russell yelped, rubbing his head. "Sorry!"

"Russell?" the voice asked in amazement.

Russell looked up – and got the surprise of his life. Somehow, he'd run right into Captain Cuddles! As the elegant European polecat reached out a paw to help Russell up, the hedgehog scrambled to his feet.

Captain Cuddles had visited Day Camp a few times in the past, and he and

Pepper had discovered that they had special feelings for each other.

"*Oui*, it is I," Captain Cuddles said with a grin. "What brings you to Paris?"

The words tumbled out of Russell in a rush as he explained everything.

"My, my, my," Captain Cuddles finally said. "You have been busy!"

"I've got to tell my friends how sorry I am," Russell told him. "But I don't even know how to get back to the airport!"

"Yes, I always find myself hopelessly lost in this part of Paris," Captain Cuddles confessed. "But you could go to the top of the Eiffel Tower! From there, you would have a wonderful view of the entire city!"

As Captain Cuddles pointed, Russell turned around to look. There it was: the Eiffel Tower, in all its gracious beauty. It was awfully high…and Russell was awfully afraid of heights…

"That's a great idea," Russell told Captain Cuddles, mustering all the courage he could.

Captain Cuddles glanced around. "My owner has an appointment at the spa," he said in a low voice. "I do not think she would notice if I escorted you there."

"Thank you!" Russell exclaimed.

"I wish I could go up with you," Captain Cuddles announced when they reached the Eiffel Tower, "but I must return before my owner notices. It was so good to see you, my friend. Please say hello to everyone for me…especially Pepper."

As Captain Cuddles hurried away, Russell sneaked onto the elevator and travelled all the way to the top. When the elevator doors whooshed open, Russell crept towards the edge of the observation deck. Every last one of his quills was quivering with fear.

Find the airport, he reminded himself. *Because that's the key to finding my friends.*

As Russell scanned the sky, he missed Paris's transformation into the City of Lights; one by one, the streetlights turned on, followed by lights in all the buildings. But there were some lights that Russell simply couldn't miss: the ones illuminating the Eiffel Tower. The brightness of the spotlights nearly blinded Russell, making him hold on to the railing for dear life as they bathed the Eiffel Tower in brilliant white light.

I can't see! Russell thought in terror as he shook his head and blinked, trying to get his vision back. A wave of dizziness washed over him.

Russell might not have been able to see, but he could still hear. Was that the *chop-chop-chop* of a helicopter?

And was it getting closer?

Russell turned his head towards the sky as the sound got louder and louder. Then, to his amazement, he thought he heard his name.

"Russell!"

That voice was so familiar…

"Blythe?" Russell yelled to the sky.

"Hang on, Russell!" Blythe cried. "We're coming!"

Hanging on – as tight as he could!

– was just about all that Russell could manage. But inside, his heart was full of joy. *They came for me,* Russell thought happily. *My friends are here!*

Slowly, as his vision began to return, Russell could make out the shape of the helicopter as it descended.

To Russell's astonishment, a ladder unfurled from the helicopter's entrance. And there was Blythe, looking pale but determined as she began to climb down it in her search-and-rescue outfit!

When their eyes met, Blythe gave Russell an encouraging smile. "This is as close as we can get!" she shouted over the noise of the helicopter. "Do you think you can jump into my arms?"

"I – I – " Russell stammered.

"I know you can do it!" Blythe told him. "On three. One…two…three!"

Russell took a deep breath, scrunched his eyes closed –

And jumped!

The night air rushed past his face, ruffling his quills as Russell flew through the air. Then, just when he thought he wasn't going to make it, Russell felt Blythe's arms wrap tightly around him.

Russell breathed a jagged sigh of relief. Cuddled in Blythe's arms was the only place he wanted to be!

As the helicopter lifted into the sky, someone inside it pulled the ladder up, up, up, until Blythe and Russell were able to hoist themselves inside. Then everyone began to cheer and celebrate!

"How?" Russell asked breathlessly, as

his friends surrounded him for high fives and hugs. "How did you ever know I was at the top of the Eiffel Tower?"

"It was the lights," Blythe explained. "As soon as they turned on, there was a giant hedgehog-shaped shadow for the entire city to see."

"You guys are the best!" Russell exclaimed, beaming. Then his smile faded a little.

"I'm so sorry," he began. "About everything! I got so carried away with Project Funway being perfect, that I forgot it was supposed to be fun... for all of us. Can you guys forgive me?"

"Of course!" Blythe said right away, as all the other pets nodded their heads, smiling. "Forgiven... and forgotten."

"Phew!" Russell breathed another sigh of relief. "That's the best news I've heard all day! And speaking of news – guess what, Pepper? I saw Captain Cuddles, and he asked me to tell you hello!"

"Really?" Pepper shrieked happily as her knees went wobbly.

Just then, Marc the photographer turned around to talk to Blythe. "I captured the entire rescue! Mona is going to be thrilled!" he announced.

"Fantastic!" Blythe replied. "Hopefully that means she won't be too angry at us for missing the show."

"Oh, she's not angry at all," Marc replied. "I just texted her to say that we're on our way back. Mona had already decided to swap the order of the event

– awards first, fashion show last. So there should be just enough time to get everyone onto the runway!"

"Really?" Blythe squealed. "Project Funway is *on*!"

After Roger landed the helicopter, Blythe and the pets sprinted towards the tent.

"Hurry!" Blythe said anxiously, as she rushed to get Russell into his outfit.

"Hey there, sweetheart," Roger said, as he touched Blythe's shoulder. "Enjoy this moment – your moment. You've earned it."

Blythe pressed her

hand over her heart as she smiled at her dad. "Thanks, Dad, you're right. We've earned it," she said. Then – suddenly – it was time for Project Funway to begin!

Zoe pranced onto the catwalk first, dressed as a doctor in a white coat with rhinestone buttons and a glittering stethoscope around her neck. Next came Minka, wearing a fantastic firefighter outfit highlighted with reflective ribbons. She burst onto the runway between two enormous fireballs – a fantastic special effect that made the crowd gasp!

The lighting suddenly shifted colour, casting blue lights against the tinsel backdrop, making it seem like everyone was underwater – the perfect effect for Vinnie and Sunil as they marched down the runway in their sea-search uniforms, complete with bright brass buttons.

Red and blue strobe lights flashed as Pepper appeared, dressed as a police officer in a black-and-white uniform with a cool reflective stripe that perfectly complemented her fur. Penny Ling came next, wearing a fashion-forward yet functional pilot's uniform. Fans blew at full power as acrobats leaped through the air above her, simulating a rescue scene. The crowd went wild – and Russell realised something. All the unique and unusual ideas his friends had had for the show hadn't ruined it.

They'd made it amazing!

"We're up next!" Blythe whispered in Russell's ear. They adjusted their matching search-and-rescue uniforms. As the star models from *Tres Blasé*'s best-selling issue, Mona Autumn had insisted that they close the show.

"Let's do it!" Russell said excitedly.

Every single person in the tent burst into wild applause when Blythe and Russell appeared.

Suddenly, Blythe's voice rang through the tent – even though she wasn't speaking.

"Russell! Russell! Hang on, Russell! We're coming!"

Blythe and Russell looked around in confusion. At the same time, they realized what was happening: Mona Autumn was showing the dramatic video footage of Blythe rescuing Russell from the top of the Eiffel Tower!

When it was over, the audience's cheers and applause shook the tent!

Mona Autumn strode onto the runway and stood next to Blythe and Russell. "Everyday heroes are everywhere," she announced. "Including our very own Blythe Baxter, who has shown us that 'daring and dramatic' doesn't just describe today's finest fashions – but the heroes who are always ready to help others!"

It didn't seem possible, but somehow the applause grew even louder. Russell and Blythe beamed, enjoying every moment in the spotlight together. When it was over, they hurried to the VIP area where their friends were waiting.

"Tomorrow we'll have to explore Paris together," said Russell. "But for now, let's get to the after-party... I don't know about you, but I am ready for some fun!"

The End

Read on for a sneak peek
of the next exciting
Littlest Pet Shop adventure,

Art from the Heart

Minka the monkey burst into the Littlest
Pet Shop, chattering with excitement as
her owner dropped her off. She stood
in the middle of the store and shook
wildly, sending droplets of water
scattering throughout the room. And
no wonder – it was pouring with rain
outside!

Still chattering, Minka catapulted
through the curtain that separated Day

Camp from the rest of the store and skidded to a sudden stop. Something was wrong – very wrong. Sure, it was dark and stormy outside…but why did her friends' faces look so dark and stormy, too?

Fashion fanatic Zoe was organising her nail polish dejectedly.

Russell the hedgehog, normally a bustling bundle of energy, was staring out of the window, absent-mindedly tallying bolts of lightning.

Penny Ling, the gentle panda, was muttering to herself as she attempted to thread a needle.

Even Pepper the skunk, who could turn just about anything into a joke, looked glum as she sprawled across a pet bed and stared at the ceiling.

Well, this is no good, Minka thought. Where are Vinnie and Sunil? They'll know how to brighten things up.

Minka found Vinnie the gecko and Sunil the mongoose in front of the TV, battling over the remote control.

"It's my turn to choose the show!" hollered Sunil.

"No, it's my turn!" Vinnie shot back.

Uh-oh, Minka thought.

Just then – sproing!

The back of the remote flew off, and four small batteries zinged through the air.

Crack! One of the batteries hit the nail polish in Zoe's paw, shattering the glass bottle.

"No!" Zoe howled. "Ravenous Red is my favourite!"

Zip! Another battery knocked the needle right out of Penny Ling's paw.

"Oh, come on!" the panda groaned

Bonk! The third battery bounced off Russell's head.

"Ow!" yelped the hedgehog.

Zoom! The fourth and final battery flew straight at Minka – but with a little quick thinking, she was able to grab it.

Zzzap! At that moment, the lights went out. The storm had knocked out the power, leaving seven pets in a dark room with nothing to do.

Everybody groaned at once – everybody except Minka.

Mrs Twombly poked her head through the curtain. "Goodness, that's a big storm out there!" she cried. "But I'm sure the power will be back on in no time. And Blythe will be here soon!"

All the pets adored Blythe Baxter – and she also had a very special talent. Blythe could actually understand the animals when they spoke, instead of just hearing barks and growls and squawks and squeaks.

Minka turned to face her friends. "What's going on?" she asked. "Why are we letting a little rain ruin our day?"

"But Minka, there's nothing to do," replied Zoe. "It's raining too hard to go to the park…"

"And it's too dark to read…" added Russell.

"That doesn't mean we can't have fun!" Minka insisted.

But what could they do in a dark Day Camp while a tremendous thunderstorm raged outside?

Suddenly, inspiration struck.

"Glow tag!" Minka shrieked. "I have this great glow-in-the-dark paint, and it comes in loads of colours, so we can each have a colour to put on our hands – or, um, paws…"

"Or sticky webbed feet!" Vinnie said.

"Or sticky webbed feet. Then we all run around in the dark and try to tag each other."

"Ooh, that sounds really fun!" exclaimed Pepper.

"But messy," Russell added.

"Don't worry about that," Minka reassured him. "We can wear our old T-shirts from the Petwalk Fundraiser last year, and play in the grooming station. Everybody, go get your T-shirts!" Minka announced. "I'll grab my paints."

It wasn't easy to find everything they needed in the dark, but they were so eager to play glow tag that soon everybody was ready.

"Line up over here," Minka told her

friends.

"Over where?" asked Vinnie.

"I can't see a thing!" Sunil said.

"Hang on, everybody!" Russell announced. "I've got a flashlight."

Click! Just like that, the pets could see where they needed to stand.

Minka twirled a paintbrush. "Who's first?"

"I'll go!" Pepper exclaimed.

Minka pranced over to Pepper and painted some neon green paint on her paws.

"Done!" Minka announced. "Russell, turn off the flashlight for a second, would you?"

"Sure," Russell replied. Suddenly the grooming station was pitch black — except for Pepper's glowing paws.

"That's awesome!" Pepper exclaimed.

Working as quickly as she could, Minka painted each pet's paws a different colour.

"With glow tag, nobody's 'it'," Minka explained. "The goal is for everybody to tag as many pets as you can. On your mark – get set – go!"

Read
Art from the Heart
to find out what happens next!

Turn the page for a special surprise from Blythe!

Welcome!

Hey, Pet Shop friends,

My pet pals and I have put together some fantastic activity pages for you!

Turn the page to discover all sorts of fun puzzles and word games.

We hope you enjoy it. See you next time at the Littlest Pet Shop!

Love,

Blythe
X

Favourite Clothes

**Ever think about putting on a fashion show of your own?
Make a list of all your favourite clothes that you
would include!**

_____

_____

_____

_____

_____

_____

_____

Wordsearch

Six words from the Project Funway story are hidden inside this grid. Can you find them all?

M	F	A	S	H	I	O	N
A	C	O	U	T	U	R	E
G	R	I	N	R	O	A	P
A	U	H	W	N	P	E	Y
Z	N	S	A	Y	T	P	T
I	W	A	Y	J	K	I	H
N	A	F	E	Y	M	A	G
E	Y	T	S	I	R	A	P

FASHION   PARIS   PET JET

MAGAZINE   COUTURE   RUNWAY

Doggy Designs

Zoe loves dressing up! Draw her a fabulous new outfit to wear at her next fashion show.

Mongoose Masterpiece

Copy each square into the grid below to create a fabulous fashion portrait for Sunil.

Pet Parts

Can you match these pets with their close-up?
Draw a line to connect each one.

Fashion Fact File

What are your favourite fashion tips and trends? Fill in these pages with your most important style info.

Draw a picture of yourself wearing your favourite outfit!

My top 5 favourite
outfits are...

1
2
3
4
5

My top 5 style
icons are...

1
2
3
4
5

My signature
hairdo is...

My favourite
accessory is...

My top colour combinations are…

My favourite fashion tip is…

My worst-ever fashion disaster was…

Minka's Maze

Minka has set up an obstacle course for Russell.
Can you help him find his way through the
maze to his friend?

FINISH

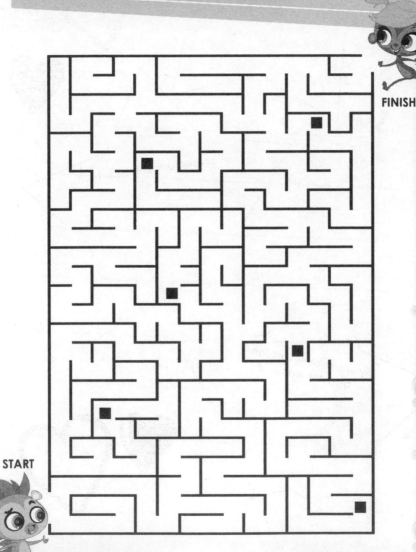

START

Sassy Style

How many fashion items beginning with S can you name? We have done the first two to start you off.

Shoes

Scarf

Vinnie Vision

Can you spot 5 differences between these 2 pictures of Vinnie?

Pepper Power

One of these pictures of Pepper is different from the others! Can you spot which one?